The Fearless Schoolboy

Books by Delshad Karanjia

Teaching a Horse to Sing: Tales of Uncommon Sense from India and Elsewhere

Akbar and Birbal: The Finest Stories of the Emperor and His Wise Minister

The Fearless Schoolboy

Four Tales of Mullah Nasruddin

DELSHAD KARANJIA

Illustrations by Mohit Suneja

ALEPH

ALEPH

ALEPH BOOK COMPANY
An independent publishing firm
promoted by ***Rupa Publications India***

First published in India in 2025
by Aleph Book Company
7/16 Ansari Road, Daryaganj
New Delhi 110 002

ISBN: 978-93-6523-586-9

1 3 5 7 9 10 8 6 4 2

Printed in India

Cha and Chat

Following a long and chequered career as a cleric, teacher, grocer, donkey driver, ferryman, water diviner, and marriage counsellor, Mullah Nasruddin decided that the time had come for him to give up full-time work and spend more time with his family. Within just a few days, he realized that being in a confined space with his wife and children was not good for his and more so their sanity. He therefore took to whiling away his time at the neighbourhood teahouse, much to his family's relief.

The teahouse, Time for Tea, was located on one of his hometown Aksehir's main thoroughfares and provided a convenient meeting place for the town's menfolk. A modest one-storey structure with a thatched roof, Time for Tea's owner had his living quarters and kitchen at one end of the house and had converted the hall and dining area into a tea room and eatery with long wooden tables and benches, where patrons spent hours in lively discussions on every subject under the sun. Three long tables and benches were arranged in a U shape against the walls, the seating arrangements facilitating conversation and interaction between customers. Visitors—regulars or strangers—happily sat at a table with other customers instead of choosing to sit on their own. In those simpler and friendlier times, people enjoyed each other's company and always made time for cha and chat.

Like Nasruddin, most of the patrons of the teahouse were in their dotage—that twilight zone in which each had less to look forward to and more to look back on—and derived great pleasure in debating the issues of the day or discussing their favourite topic:

themselves. Most of the teahouse's patrons had grown up in and around Aksehir, and had known each other for more than four decades. Nasruddin was by far the town's most famous son, having gained a reputation for fearlessly questioning authority and outsmarting renowned thinkers. It was, therefore, not surprising that the mullah often did most of the talking and also featured prominently in his friends' nostalgic stories.

Over steaming cups of tea, Nasruddin's childhood friend Hussain was reminiscing about their schooldays. 'It's hard to imagine that the mullah, now considered a pillar of our community, was once the bane of our schoolteachers. He was defiant, disobedient, and completely unafraid of the punishments he received,' Hussain began.

'Although Nasruddin was famous for defying and outwitting our teacher, his biggest fightback was with a fellow student. I remember one incident as if it happened yesterday. We must have been around eleven years of age when a few of us, Nasruddin included, were being badgered and bullied by an older student named Talah, who was not only stronger than us, but also came from a much wealthier family. He scoffed at our worn, patched-up clothes and scruffy footwear, and said he felt sorry for us because we would never amount to anything in life.'

Pausing for a sip of tea, Hussain continued: 'Our first response to the bully was to ignore him, but he mistook our silence for fear, and troubled us even more. One day, Nasruddin decided to confront our tormentor....

'He went straight up to Talah and said: "You're a bully and a coward, picking on kids who cannot or won't fight back. Just because you wear smarter clothes and have more money than us doesn't make you better than us, nor does it give you the right to keep putting us down like this. If *you* had earned the money that enabled you to buy all your finery, your shameful boasting would be understandable, but

still inexcusable." Talah just stood there, speechless, so Nasruddin continued even more confidently.

'"As I see it, my friends and I are better off being insignificant nobodies rather than an arrogant somebody like you. It's sad that the only way you can feel superior is by making others look inferior." And with that, Nasruddin turned and walked away, leaving the bully stunned, opening and closing his mouth like a fish out of water, still unable to speak. Needless to say, we had no problems with Talah from then on.'

The hushed silence at the end of Hussain's story was broken by cries of 'Vay be! Vay be! Well done! Well done!'

from patrons of the teahouse.

'What I learned from that experience is that bullies are cowards and once you confront them, they're too scared to fight back,' Nasruddin said, openly delighted with the vocal acclaim for his bravery.

'I wonder what happened to Talah,' one of the townsfolk mused aloud.

'I heard that he fell into bad company,' Abdul, a local landowner and moneylender, spoke up. 'Talah squandered his father's wealth, got heavily into debt, and borrowed money from friends and relatives, none of whom were paid back. When his creditors—myself included—began baying for his blood, we were told that Talah had abandoned his wife and family and run off to Constantinople. He has not been seen in these parts since.'

'Good riddance,' the learned mullah exclaimed. 'How people behave after they have borrowed money from you reveals a great deal about their character or lack thereof.'

'I agree with you completely, Nasruddin,' Abdul interjected. 'I'm amazed how many people seem to completely forget about the money they've borrowed from me, forcing me to remind them about the loan. When I ask them to repay me, they take great offence and get angry with me for asking them for my money!'

Nasruddin nodded and said: 'It's never a good idea to borrow money, and even worse to lend it. Sadly, whenever I've needed money, people have been most reluctant to lend me any. I often wonder why people seem more willing to dole out money to the greedy rather than the needy.'

No Shortage of Advice

The learned mullah liked to spend a lot of his time outdoors, not because he loved nature especially, but more to escape his wife Fatima's ceaseless demands that he help her around the house.

The family member whose company he seemed to enjoy most was that of his son, Ahmed, a quiet and diffident boy who had been henpecked into docility by his domineering mother and two older sisters—quite the opposite effect that Nasruddin's mother and sisters had had on him. As soon as Ahmed was old enough, Nasruddin cajoled the boy into accompanying him on his eventful forays with his donkey Akilli to markets in neighbouring towns.

One warm summer's day, with Ahmed riding on Akilli's back and Nasruddin walking alongside holding the reins, the trio set off on their shopping expedition as fast as the little grey donkey's temperamental pace would allow. They were plodding along happily when they came across a troupe of dervishes, instantly recognizable in their flowing white robes, who were on their way to a cultural festival in Aksehir. The dervishes bowed their heads in respectful greeting to Nasruddin, but one member of the group glowered at Ahmed, shook his head disapprovingly, and said: 'You should be ashamed of yourself, young man. You are healthy and strong and yet

you sit astride a donkey while your elderly father, who looks feeble and fatigued, is forced to walk! It is a sorry state of affairs that the youth of today show no consideration for their elders.'

'There's no need to get into such a whirl,' Nasruddin mumbled, deeply offended at being called elderly and feeble. Ahmed, humiliated by this exchange, dismounted immediately and insisted that his father ride Akilli while he walked alongside.

Everything went well for a while and the threesome were trudging along at a fair pace with Nasruddin riding his donkey, facing backwards, and chatting casually with his son when they came across a group of women sitting and gossiping by the roadside. The women's conversation died down when they spotted the father, son, and the little donkey. As the trio approached them, the women hastily covered their faces with their veils,

tut-tutted in dismay, and one of them said loud enough for the passers-by to hear: 'Isn't it disgraceful that the father rides comfortably on the donkey and makes the young child walk in this heat? Parents have become so uncaring these days....'

Now it was Nasruddin's turn to be embarrassed. He lifted Ahmed up to ride along with him and they proceeded on their journey, hoping against hope that they would not encounter any more advice-givers on the way. Unfortunately, that was not to be.

At the very next village, several residents gave the father and son disapproving looks and bemoaned the

fate of the poor donkey: 'What heartless and selfish people,' one of the villagers said. 'Father and son both look perfectly

hale and hearty, yet they're both riding on one tiny donkey. The poor creature looks ready to collapse under their weight!'

On hearing this, father and son both dismounted immediately and decided to continue their journey on foot. 'That should put an end to all unsolicited advice,' fumed an infuriated Nasruddin, but he had spoken too soon.

They had gone only a short distance when a group of men laughed out loud at the sight of the father, son, and donkey walking past them. 'Just look at those buffoons,' they scoffed. 'They prefer to walk in the heat despite having a strong and sturdy donkey they could easily ride! It's clear that the most senseless of the three is not the one you'd expect it to be!'

Nasruddin was stung by the men's

insults. I hadn't realized that Akilli had such a large family, with so many loud-mouthed supporters, he thought to himself. Then trying to make the best of a bad situation, he turned to Ahmed and smiled: 'Son, we've learned an important lesson today, which is that people have opinions—especially on matters that don't concern them—and seldom hesitate to voice them. They would have criticized us even if we had been carrying Akilli instead of the other way round! There's a saying that everyone has two eyes but no one has the same view. The point is that no matter how hard one tries, one can never ever please everyone.'

'If that's the case, Baba, were we

wrong to let other people's opinions influence us?' the boy asked.

'No, we were not wrong nor were they right,' Nasruddin replied. 'But sometimes, for the sake of peace, it is better to heed other people's views. If we all choose to ignore everyone else and do as we please, there would be chaos in the world.'

Preacher's Block

One of Nasruddin's regular preoccupations was to give religious discourses and lead the Friday prayers at one of the town's mosques. A recent addition to the town's landscape, the wooden-roofed mosque in the mullah's charge was a more modest structure than the ancient mosque with the imposing minaret that had greatly impressed him in his childhood. The new mosque had a smaller dome and a shorter minaret but boasted a spacious prayer hall and wooden pillars adorned with intricately carved geometric designs.

Having grown immune to the mosque's aesthetic appeal and having preached there every Friday for years on end, the mullah was running out of original ideas for his sermons and yearned for a break. One hot summer's day, not having given any thought to the topic of his sermon, he climbed up to the pulpit, surveyed his congregation seated on the plush carpet on the tiled floor looking up at him intently, and asked: 'Do you know the subject I'm going to discuss today?'

'No,' came the honest reply, as his followers shook their heads in confusion.

'How can you not know, given all the major events that have occurred in the past week? I am not going to waste my time preaching to such an ignorant assembly,' said Nasruddin indignantly, then flounced out of the mosque and headed home for a siesta.

The following Friday, he climbed up to the pulpit and asked the same question: 'Oh, ye men of faith, do you know the subject of my sermon today?'

Fearful of offending the mullah and causing a repeat of the walkout that had been staged the week before, the congregation nodded their heads and replied: 'Yes, yes. We know what you are going to discuss today.'

'In that case, there is no point in my telling you what you already know,' said the mullah, making another hasty exit.

The next week, Nasruddin again climbed up to the minbar and asked the congregation: 'Do you know what I'm going to speak about today?'

This time, his followers had anticipated the question and were well prepared with their answer. 'Some of us know and some do not,' they said.

'That's good. Then those who know can tell those who don't,' said the mullah and left.

Tiring of their mullah's idiosyncrasies,

the congregation agreed that something should be done. After some deliberation, they appointed a village elder to have a stern word with the mullah. Woken from his afternoon snooze by someone knocking at his door, Nasruddin was surprised to see the town's oldest resident. 'Please come in,' said Nasruddin, trying hard not to look as if he'd been asleep.

'Thank you,' the man replied. 'I'm here merely to pass on a message from the members of your congregation. Having missed out on your enlightening sermons for three weeks in a row, the villagers are considering inviting a mullah from a nearby village to lead the Friday prayers for a couple of weeks to give you a bit

of a break. I'm sure you will welcome their decision.'

Realizing that the townsfolk had seen through his trickery, and terrified of losing his job and his stature in the community, Nasruddin quickly replied: 'Please inform the villagers that there is no need to find a substitute mullah while I am alive. Assure them that I will be there next week and the topic of my sermon will be the importance of regularly attending Friday prayers.'

Planning Ahead

Nasruddin took up a part-time job as assistant to a trader who ran a prosperous business in Aksehir, but the mullah's absentminded and erratic behaviour sometimes proved too much for his employer. One day, the trader lost his temper.

'Nasruddin,' he yelled, 'why don't you try using your brains once in a while?

Why must you make three trips to the market to buy three eggs? Why can't you buy all three eggs in a single trip? You've made a habit of not completing your tasks in one go. You're wasting your time and my money because of your foolish ways. Is it too much to ask that you complete all your errands in one trip?'

Realizing that his employer was at the end of his tether and that he might lose a lucrative job, Nasruddin acknowledged his mistake. 'Please forgive me, sir. From now on, I will follow your instructions and not waste time going back and forth to complete my assigned tasks. All my jobs will be completed in one trip, I assure you.'

A week later, the trader suddenly took ill and instructed Nasruddin to fetch the hakim as soon as possible. Nasruddin bustled off on his bandy legs and returned a short while later at the head of a small procession of men. Walking briskly behind Nasruddin was Arif, the local hakim, and behind him came a man carrying a wooden box full of tiny vials of medicine, followed by four men, one of whom was carrying a white shroud and another a wreath.

Perplexed at the sight of this parade, the trader asked weakly: 'What is the meaning of this, Nasruddin? Who are all these people?'

Nasruddin replied: 'I fetched the

hakim as you requested. I also asked the apothecary to come along so he can provide whatever medication Arif prescribes. I hope and pray that you recover after his treatment. But in case you don't get better and the worst happens, I have made arrangements for these pallbearers to take you to the cemetery. I followed your instructions and completed all tasks in one trip.'

Nasruddin's employer was dazed and dumbstruck but felt too ill to argue against his employee's undeniable logic.